Jonathan James

and the

Whatif Monster

Michelle Nelson-Schmidt

Kane Miller

A DIVISION OF EDC PUBLISHING

For my amazing parents, Mike and Sylvia
- who always encouraged me to be myself,
despite their worries and "what ifs."

Kane Miller, A Division of EDC Publishing

Text and illustrations copyright © Michelle Nelson-Schmidt 2012

For information contact:
Kane Miller, A Division of EDC Publishing
PO Box 470663
Tulsa, OK 74147-0663
www.kanemiller.com
www.edcpub.com
www.usbornebooksandmore.com

Library of Congress Control Number: 2011945335

Manufactured by Regent Publishing Services, Hong Kong
Printed June 2016 in ShenZhen, Guangdong, China

Hardcover ISBN: 978-1-61067-131-6
Paperback ISBN: 978-1-61067-118-7

Some Whatif Monsters like to hang out,
and fill up our heads with worry and doubt.

They are sneaky and quiet and quick as a blink,
the words that they whisper can change how we think.

Jonathan James heard those words full of dread,
and all those "what ifs" got stuck in his head.

What if you tumble?
What if there's wind?
What if you slip, and your knee
gets all skinned?

What if they giggle?
What if it's chilly?
What if you jump
and look really silly?

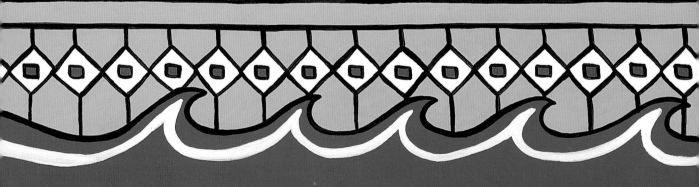

What if it's hard?
What if you're bad?
What if they laugh and
make you feel sad?

What if it's ugly? What if it stinks?
What if that's what *everyone* thinks?

What if it's yucky? What if it's icky?
What if Mom yells because you're too picky?

What if it's dark? What if it's scary?
What if there's something giant and hairy?

What if you lose? What if you're last?
What if you're slow and never get fast?

What if she laughs? What if she runs?
What if she thinks you're not any fun?

"Now wait just a minute! I have something to say, after hearing 'what ifs' all through the day. I hear all your worries; I hear all your claims. But what if you're wrong?" asks Jonathan James.

What if I climb to the *top* of that tree,
and I never slip or skin up a knee?

And what if I jump right into that pool,
and everyone thinks I look really *cool*?

And what if baseball is nothing but *fun*,
and I end up hitting a triple home run?

And what if my drawing goes up on the wall,
and everyone thinks it's the *best* one of all?

And what if I taste
some of that food,
and it puts my mouth
in a really *good* mood?

And what if I run in a really
big race, and have a *great*
time no matter what place?

And what if I sleep and have
the best dream ...
that monsters are *sweeter*
than they all seem?

And what if the chance I take in the end,

is just how I find my very *best* friend?